An I Can Read Book™

Baa-Choo!

by Sarah Weeks
pictures by Jane Manning

HarperCollins*Publishers*

HarperCollins®, 🐾®, and I Can Read Book®
are trademarks of HarperCollins Publishers Inc.

Baa-Choo!
Text copyright © 2004 by Sarah Weeks
Illustrations copyright © 2004 by Jane Manning
Printed in the U.S.A.
www.harperchildrens.com

Library of Congress Cataloging-in-Publication Data
Weeks, Sarah.
  Baa-choo! / by Sarah Weeks ; illustrated by Jane Manning.— 1st ed.
  p. cm. — (An I can read book)
  Summary: When Sam the lamb has trouble sneezing, the other animals try to help.
  ISBN 0-06-029236-9 — ISBN 0-06-029237-7 (lib. bdg.)
  [1. Sneezing—Fiction. 2. Sheep—Fiction. 3. Domestic animals—Fiction. 4. Stories in rhyme.] I. Manning, Jane K., ill. II. Title. III. Series.
PZ8.3.W4125Bae 2004
[E]—dc22

                                                                    2003017549

1 2 3 4 5 6 7 8 9 10
❖
First Edition

For my dear friend Janet
—S.W.

For Hilary, Emily, and Mallory—
three sweet girls who never sneeze!
—J.M.

"I've got a cold,"

said Sam the lamb.

"I'm going to sneeze,

indeed I am."

His little nose twitched,

and wiggled,

and itched.

"Baa . . . ahh . . ."

No *choo*.

"I've got the *ahhh*

but not the *choo*.

No, no, this sneeze

will never do."

9

"Can someone help me,
help me please,
to find the ending
of my sneeze?"

"I'll tickle your nose
with a feather, and then
I'm sure you'll sneeze,"
said Gwen the hen.

11

She tickled his nose.

Sam said,

"Here goes!

Baa . . . ahhh . . ."

No *choo*.

"Gee," said Sam.

"That didn't feel right.

It felt . . . almost,

but then . . . not quite.

14

"Can someone help me,

help me please,

to find the ending

of my sneeze?"

Sig the pig said,

"I have a plan.

We'll sprinkle some pepper

in front of this fan.

"Sam, stand over there,

and stick out your nose,

and sniff wherever

the pepper blows."

17

So Sam sniffed,

and snorted,

and snuffed.

Huffed and puffed

with his nose all stuffed.

The pepper went flying.

Sam kept trying.

"Baa . . . ahhh . . ."

No *choo*.

"Gee," said Sam.

"This isn't much fun.

Why can't this sneeze

be over and done?

"Can someone help me,
help me please,
to find the ending
of my sneeze?"

Franny Nannygoat

came by

and said that she

would like to try.

"I'll kick up dust!"

And so she did,

with a bit of help

from her little kid.

The dust was thick.

Sam started to wheeze,

and then at last

he started to sneeze.

This time it was bigger.

And louder and longer.

Instead of stopping,

it just got stronger.

"Quick! Everyone do
whatever you can!"
Gwen grabbed her feather.
Sig turned on his fan.

Together they tickled
and sprinkled and kicked
to make the big sneeze grow.
Then someone cried,
"Look out! Look out!
I think he's going to blow!"

Then Sam the lamb
let out a sneeze
that raised the roof
and shook the trees.

Believe me when
I say it's true,
no lamb has sneezed
a louder *choo*.

29

"Thank you, friends,"

said Sam the lamb,

"for coming to the rescue."

Sam heard them say,

from far away,

"You're welcome, Sam, and—"

"Bless you!"